ZOEY
WONDERS WHY

Nadia Khan

ISBN: 979-8-9856400-0-7 (hardback)

ISBN: 979-8-9856400-1-4 (paperback)

ISBN: 979-8-9856400-2-1 (ebook)

Cover design and illustrations by Tasya Nabiella.

Printed in the U.S.A.

Dedication

Dear Aadam, Haroon, Zaki, and Musa,

I wrote this story for you boys to know that all that you are is what you make yourself to be. Everything about you, your likes, dislikes, and your unique way of seeing things in life make you the best to Daddy and me. I created this book to help you and the readers understand that it's okay to be different, and you shouldn't be afraid to step out from your comfort zone and explore things that you may have never imagined. Be like Zoey; be true to yourself, and share your kindness and caring characteristics to the world. The world belongs to children who see life as a big storybook, ready to be enjoyed. I hope you children, and my readers, enjoy Zoey as much as I enjoyed creating her.

Love,
Your mom,
Nadia

Contents

Meaning of Words

Gulab Jamun: A South Asia sweet dessert of fried dough dipped in a sugar syrup with rose water.

Biryani: A rice dish eaten in South Asia that is slowly cooked with spices, onions, tomatoes, and some form of meat, such as chicken, goat, or beef.

Butter Chicken: A chicken dish eaten in South Asia made with spices, butter, and chicken in a creamy tomato sauce.

Daal: Lentils eaten in South Asia as a staple dish. It is paired with bread or eaten with rice.

Raita: A yogurt dish eaten in South Asia made with shredded cucumbers, mint, and a hint of spices if needed.

Bigos Stew: Hunters stew is native to Poland and is made of chopped meat, sauerkraut, and additional shredded cabbage. It is served with vegetables, spices, and wine.

Perogies: Dumplings filled with salty fillings such as potatoes and onions, or they can be sweet too. They are boiled, then pan-fried, and served hot. They are native to Poland and Eastern European countries.

Pounded Yams: An African dish that is like mashed potatoes and served with soup.

Jollof Rice: A rice dish native to West Africa made with rice, tomatoes, onions, and spices. It is paired with some form of meat, sometimes chicken.

Rusk Cake: A twice-baked bread native to South Asia that is eaten at teatime.

Chai: A black tea made with sugar and milk or cream. Some variations use cardamom or cinnamon.

Aloo: The South Asian word for potatoes.

Samosa: A South Asian dish that is fried or baked with a salty or sweet filling. It is eaten as an appetizer. It is in the shape of a triangle and served hot with chai.

Badaam: Almonds in South Asia.

Cheeni: Sugar in South Asia.

Namaz: Ritual prayers performed by people in specific religions such as Christians, Muslims, Hindus, Buddhists, Zoroastrians, etc.

Nihari: A beef stew that is slowly cooked with spices and tomatoes served as a main dish in South Asia.

Shahi Tukray: Butter-fried bread pieces cooked in sweetened milk with nuts and saffron. It is a sweet dish made in South Asia with a Persian influence. It literally translates to "a royal piece of dessert."

CHAPTER 1
Zoey's Cultural Project

Hi, friend! I'm Zoey; I just turned five. Are you five, too, friend? Guess what? I'm starting school this month. Which month, might you ask? September! (Sep-tem-BRR.) That's in the summer season, not fall, silly-boo. 😊 Yeah, it's hard for me too.

I love September because my favorite season starts. Yes, you're right, it's fall! Do you know why I love fall? I get to jump in a mountain of leaves. I can scare my baby brothers from the pile, like an orange-striped monster, hehehe!

I'm a big sister and a big helper too! Are you? I help Mommy, Daddy, Zaky, and my smallest brother, Max. I don't have a dog or a cat. I would want a puppy that could fit in the pocket of my red jacket so I could take it to school. Sigh … Time to be good at school; Mommy and Daddy might get me one!

Let's go home, friend. It's time for dinner. Mommy is here. Yay!

"Zoey," said Mom, "How is my lovebug?"

"I'm fine," I said. "Mommy, you smell yummy! What did you make?" I asked. "No more mac and cheese or yucky broccoli," I said sadly.

"Aww, sweet pea, I made your favorites: biryani, butter chicken, and daal," said Mommy.

"But, but, Mommy … Dessert?" I asked.

"You will just have to wait and see, sweetie," said Mommy.

I went inside my home, and it was warm and filled with yummy smells of spices and, of course, dessert. "I'm going to find out what Mommy made. Let's investigate," I said. Do you want to help, friend? I'm smelling something sweet. Like … like … um … um …

"Mommy!"

"Yes, sweet pea?" said Mommy.

"Does the smell I smell have warm sugar?" I asked.

"Yes, it does, Zoey. Better yet, let's play hot or cold for you to find the yummy treats."

"Yay! Mommy, I love hot or cold."

Would you know where the smell is coming from, friend? Would you help me? Really? You will? Yay! Okay, let's close our eyes and use our noses. I walked around but reached the garbage pail and, pee yew, it stunk. Yuck!

"You're cold, love, "said Mommy.

"Hmm," I thought, "maybe somewhere warm." And I tip-toed, eyes closed, off to the oven.

Mommy stuck out her hand to push me away from the heat. "You're warm, sweetie," she said.

"Hmm..." I thought as I turned around and walked to the island. Not a real island, silly-boo friend, just an eating table that is big, I mean, huge.

"Poof," said Mommy, "You're hot, Zoey! You're burning up. Open your eyes." I opened my eyes, and to my delight, it was my most favorite dessert ever: gulab jamuns! "Thank you," I said.

13

14

"You're welcome, and enjoy," said Mommy. I sat down with my plate and bit into the sweet round-shaped goodness while it squirted out its syrup onto my plate.

"Finish up, sweetie, and wash your hands so we can get going on that homework Miss Thumsickle has given to you," said Mommy.

"This Friday, we need to bring something to share with our class about where we are from, Mommy."

"Yes, sweet pea, where are we from?" Mommy asked me.

"I'm not sure, Mommy. Daddy says he grew up in Africa, but his family is in India, and that's in Asia, right, Mommy?" I said.

"Hmm, yes, sweet pea, but you forgot about me. Where is your Mommy from?"

I thought and slowly answered with reluctance, "Mommy, you have Pakistani culture but were raised in the United States ... I'm so confused, Mommy. That is too much for me to remember for class," I cried.

"It's okay, Zoey. We will figure it out before Friday," said Mommy.

I sat quietly and ate my dinner. It was yummy chicken biryani with some raita on the side to calm the spicy. Daddy quietly watched me and, after dinner, sat me down on his lap and calmly asked, "Princess warrior? Is something on your mind?"

"No, Daddy, I'm just tired from all the work I did, and I'm just going to bed," I lied. I wanted to tell Daddy that I don't know what I am. What culture do I tell my class?

I didn't sleep well that night and tossed and turned from left to right until Mommy came in to wake me up for school.

Chapter 2
Troubles at School

At school, I met my friends, Mika and Sam. "Hi Mika and Sam," I said. "What smells so good? I'm getting hungry smelling it." The classroom smelled like warm gooey cheese with a hint of potatoes and onions.

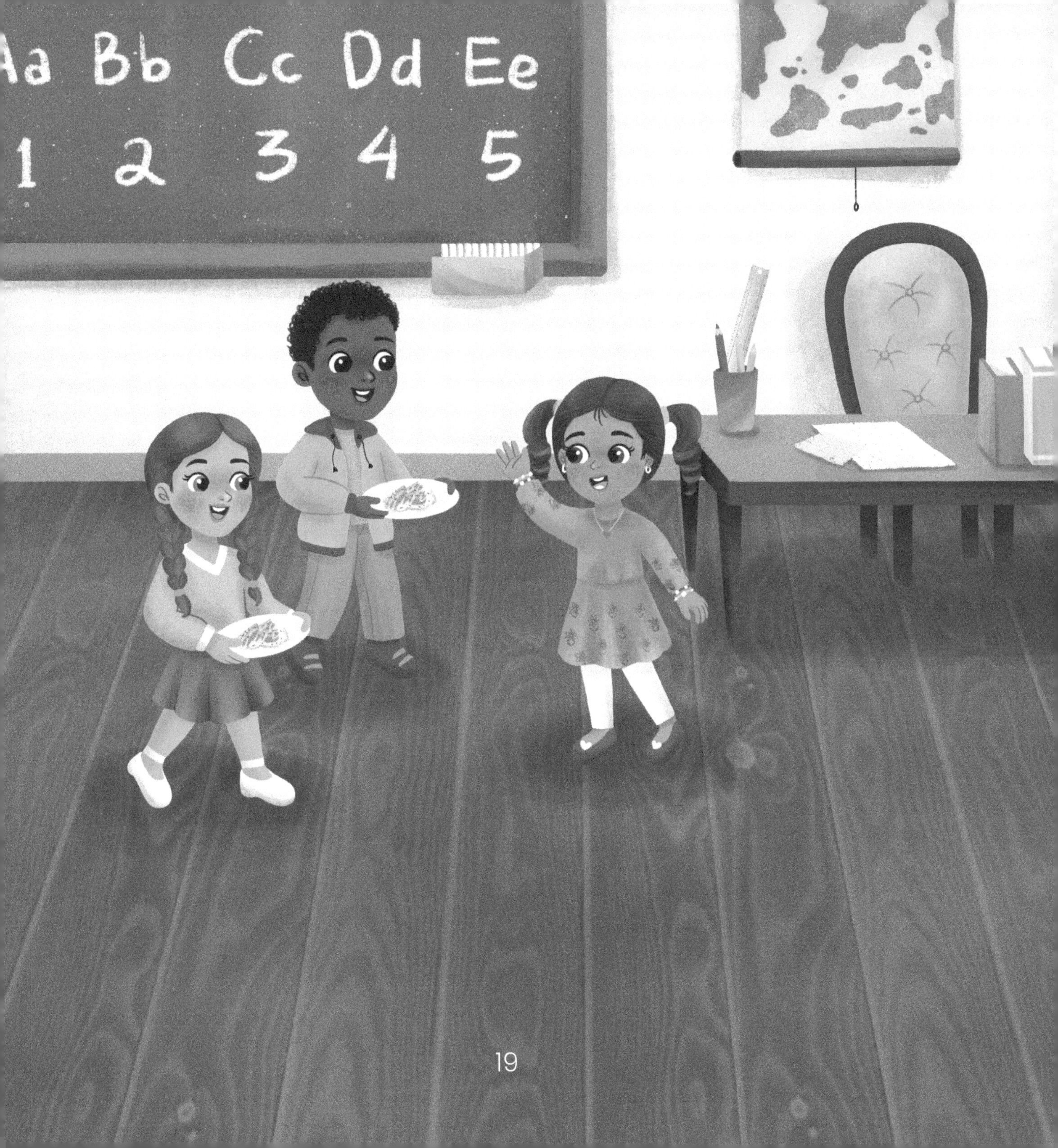
Aa Bb Cc Dd Ee
1 2 3 4 5

Class B

TOILET

20

Mika went in front of the class and said, "Good morning, friends. This is my culture and where I'm from is Poland. My family grew up far from here in East Europe. We eat bigos stew and many different types of pierogis, sweet and salty."

My tummy started to rumble like a train coming to its stop. I touched my tummy and told it, "Wait."

Sam was next. I closed my eyes and smelled similar spices to what Mommy used, and it smelled like tomato soup. I couldn't stop myself since I didn't eat much last night, and I got up from my chair. "Please, sit down, Zoey; Sam hasn't started yet," said Miss Thumsickle from beside Sam's desk.

"Sorry, Miss Thumsickle," I said, "it just smells so good."

"Hi all, my family is from a country in Africa called Nigeria, and it is in the west area of Africa," said Sam. "We eat pounded yams and jollof rice, which are everyday foods that we eat, and it is the dishes I have brought to school today."

25

Sam smiled so much you could see all his teeth. I was slowly inching out of my seat but remembered to be patient. Mika and Sam handed out their yummy food to the class, and boy, oh boy, I loved the different tastes that were having a party in my mouth. I couldn't hold my emotions and yelled, "This is so good! Thank you! The best, tastiest stuff ever."

"Shh," said Miss Thumsickle, "Zoey, what is going on with you? Please think about your friends here."

At the end of the day, Miss Thumsickle handed me a note to give to Mommy.

Chapter 3
Fearful Zoey and the note

When I got home, I gave the note to Mommy. "Hey, Zoey. What's this sweetie?" asked Mommy.

"My teacher told me to give it to you," I said. She sat down on the couch with her cup of chai and a plate of rusk cakes she made. It was still warm, and I just wanted to dunk it in Mommy's chai and gobble it all up. "Hmm, Zoey, dear, can you tell me what happened today at school?" asked Mommy.

"Um … um … um … Mommy, I kind of got too excited in class today and got up from my chair twice," I said. "Miss Thumsickle wasn't very happy, but Mommy, Mika and Sam presented their cultures, and their food smelled so good I couldn't help it."

Looking down at my knees, I continued, "Plus, I was really hungry and couldn't keep my emotions in."

"Aw, sweetie, I'm so glad you told me. Next time, keep calm, think happy thoughts, and let your friends show the class what they have."

32

Then Mommy said, "Tomorrow, it's your turn to present your dish. What should we make, sweetie?"

"I know, Mommy," I said, "Let's make samosas with aloo and rice."

"All right, let's get to it then, Zoey. Zaky and Max would love to help make samosas! Let's check if they want to join, too," said Mommy.

"Zaky! Max!" I yelled at the top of my lungs. "Do you want to help us? We are making samosas with aloo!"

34

Running down the stairs, yelling, "Yes, yes, yes!" Zaky was pulling Max in tow. I had so much fun putting and measuring the ingredients into the mixer until Zaky decided to be curious.

"Hey, the flour looks like snow!" and whoosh, he blew it at Zoey, then Max, and then Mommy.

37

"Okay, guys, let's get this cleaned up," said Mommy. We made our triangles filled with aloo and watched Mommy fry them. The whole table was full of warm-smelling samosas. "Zoey, dear, get back. Max and Zaky, you guys too," said Mommy. " I have something for you all; it's filled with a surprise," said Mommy.

"I wonder what it is," I thought. "Oh, oh, oh, I hope it has chocolate, don't you, Zaky?"

"What if it's, um, badaam with cheenee? " said Zaky, while jumping up and down with Max. I couldn't wait and pushed my way to get one, but along the way, Zaky fell, with Max falling on his face.

A loud cry came from Max. "Mommy!" Tears were rolling down his cheeks.

I put down my samosa and thought, "I'm so bad I did that to Max, and for what? Food?" I dropped what I was doing and gave my brother, Max, a hug. "I'm sorry, Max and Zaky, I just got so carried away with eating that I didn't think about either of you at all," I said.

"It's okay, Zoey," said Zaky.

"It's okay, Zzzooooeeee," said Max.

"I got chocolate," I said.

"I got almonds!" said Max and Zaky in unison.

Later that night, Mommy and Daddy were tucking me into bed. I felt very safe and warm. "Goodnight, Mommy and Daddy. Thank you, Mommy, for helping make the samosas and for not punishing me for pushing Zaky and Max. I was too busy thinking about food and not thinking about others and what's around me," I said.

"Aww, we love you, sweet pea, and we're just glad you learned something," said Mommy. Mommy and Daddy kissed me on my forehead, and I drifted off to sleep, dreaming of the big day tomorrow to present my culture to my class.

Chapter 4
Culture Showdown

The next morning, I woke up early and did my namaz before sunrise with Mommy and Daddy. I was ready to show my class who I was. I knew now what the class would learn and what I learned from everyone who presented. "Let's do this!"

43

I walked to the front of the class. "Hi friends, today I will be presenting where I am from. After watching you all, I'm very lucky to know where I'm from. My cultures are like easter eggs in a basket; all that are beautiful on their own but, as a whole, shine bright like stars."

I put out my tray of samosas and some jollof rice with a deep sigh. "I belong to a family where we are from South Asia, in India and Pakistan, and Africa, in Nigeria," I said. "We eat samosas that are filled with potatoes just like the perogies Mika showed us, and tomato rice, like Sam brought to class. We all may be different, but you know what, we are all awesome. Who wants some rice and some yummy samosas?" I asked.

45

"Me!" said everyone in the class, grabbing little plates.

When I went back home later that day, I ran and gave Mommy and Daddy a great big hug. "Daddy, Mommy, I did it! I found myself," I said. "I know that all of me is full of all the wonderful cultures that you both teach me, Zaky, and Max. Mommy, can you teach me more about the food you know how to make?" I asked. "Do we have anything like Bigos Stew that Mika presented? It tasted super yummy, and ... and... and something sweet too."

"Of course, sweetie, we have something called nihari that is super delish and sweet. Hmm … I think shahi tukray, too," said Mommy.

"That sounds so good, Mommy; let's try to make it soon," I smiled. "I promise I will be good and let Zaky and Max help too," I said.

"Deal," Mommy said.

"Deal," I said, with a high five to Mommy.

As we went inside our home, I closed the door behind me, and off I went to hear more wonderful stories from Mommy and Daddy on the different cultures they were shown when they were kids. I'd love to share more of my culture with you, and I hope you talk about your culture with your family too.

I can't wait to share more about me with you. Are you ready to join my next adventure, friend? I hope to see you again soon! Goodbye for now, friend.

Acknowledgments:

I would first want to thank my wonderful children Aadam, Haroon, Zaki, and Musa, who let me enjoy reading books and bring the magic of storytelling come to life. I thank my husband, Imran, for pushing me to do what I always loved, which was writing. I most want to thank you, the reader, for reading my book, and I hope you enjoy the stories I create.

Review Ask

Love this book? Don't forget to leave a review!

Every review matters, and it matters a lot!
Your input will help me create and design my books so that I can
bring the joy of reading about Zoey to you.
Head over to Amazon or wherever you purchased this book to
leave a review for me.
Thank you so much in advance.

Author Bio

Nadia Khan is a mother to four little boys who keep her on her toes. She has loved reading and writing ever since she was a little kid. She lives with her family in Nutley, NJ. Her favorite color is blue, and she loves baking cookies and cakes with her kids. She loves Curious George, Bluey, and Sesame Street with her kids. She is currently catching up on adult shows, Games of Thrones and Lost in Space. Nadia enjoys books in the fantasy/science fiction categories. Nadia would love that this book helps you as a parent and the readers be proud of who they are. All the readers should know they are special just the way they are. Enjoy more books to come with Zoey.

Check out my Instagram page and my website **Zoeywonderswhy.com** for more fun activities.

Free Coloring pages and activities are on the website.

Scan the QR codes for the fun to begin.

Illustrator Bio

Tasya Nabiella Buchori is from Indonesia. She is an illustrator who specializes in childrens book illustration and has a background in art education. Tasya loves to tell stories through visual, and currently she has illustrated more than 25 books from various countries. Check out her Instagram page for her work @tasyanabiella

Zoey Wonders Why

Lightning Source UK Ltd.
Milton Keynes UK
UKHW052120200422
401794UK00002B/29